I thought I heard a goldfish singing ...

by Leon Rosselson

Ilustrated by Lesley Buckingham

LONGMAN

PART ONE
Michael's Story

CHAPTER ONE
Arguments

Hello. My name's Michael. That's Michael not Mike. I'm not a Mike. It's bad enough being the littlest one in the family without being turned into a Mike. My sister's name is Ella and if you dare make jokes about Cinders or Ugly Sisters or being turned into a pumpkin, watch out for her left hook. She doesn't think they're funny. You have been warned.

Ella says I'm to tell you the first part of this strange story and how it all began one boring Sunday afternoon in the middle of the heat wave which you probably remember we had last summer holidays. We were in the coolest part of the house, the room with the television but we weren't watching it. Mum and Dad had made us switch it off because we couldn't agree on which programme to watch. They said it would teach us not to argue. Actually, since we were fed up with playing snakes and ladders, there was nothing else to do but argue.

Mum said it was the beginning of the end of the world. It was the global warming, she said, and the ice caps would soon be melting so we'd better start making an ark like Noah if we didn't all want to be drowned.

"What a misery!" said Dad. "You always think the worst. In fact, you enjoy thinking the worst. Thinking the worst is the only thing that makes you happy. Anyway, there have been plenty of summers just as hot as this before the global warming was even thought of."

"Like when?" said Mum.

"You know I can never remember dates," Dad said.

"I know you can never remember my birthday," Mum replied.

Then they started quarrelling over who should have which bit of the Sunday paper. All the windows were open so I expect the whole street was enjoying our Mum and Dad having a go at each other. We didn't mind. We were used to it. We knew that when they argued, they didn't really mean it.

Ella was lying in the middle of the floor, staring up at the ceiling. "I'm bored," she said.

"I'm boreder," I shouted from the sofa.

"I'm boredest," she shouted, louder still.

"You can't be," I said. "There's no such word as 'boredest'."

"That's all you know," Ella said.

"Well I've never heard it."

"Yes, you have, 'cos I've just used it. I'm boredest. There," she said, "you've heard it again."

I can't really argue with my sister. It's not just that

she's bigger and older than me. It's that whatever I say, even when I know I'm right, I can't ever win. She won't let me. She'll say things I don't understand just to confuse me. So I usually end up calling her names.

"You're a big fat tomato," I said, "and you ought to be squashed and turned into tomato sauce." Then I got ready to leap out of the way of her left hook but I was saved by the bell. The doorbell, that is.

"What's that?" Dad asked in an annoyed voice.

"Tell him, Ella," Mum said sarcastically. "Tell him what happens when you press the doorbell."

"I mean, who is it?" Dad said. "On a Sunday and all."

"Probably the neighbours complaining about you shouting so loud," said Mum.

"I am not shouting," shouted Dad.

The doorbell rang again.

"Isn't anyone going to answer it?" asked Dad.

"Answer the door, Ella," said Mum.

"Answer the door, Michael," said Ella.

"I have to do everything in this house," I said. But I ran to the door to see who it was because, you never know, it could have been somebody bringing me a spectacular present – like a powerful telescope to look at the moon and the stars, or a plane ticket to Cape Canaveral. It could have been something wonderful. It could have been. But it wasn't. It was . . .

CHAPTER TWO
Three Grey Men

There they were in a line on the doorstep, long, thin and grey. Their suits were grey. Their shoes were grey. Their hats were grey. Their ties were grey. Their briefcases were grey. Even their skin was grey. Grey from top to toe and everywhere in between . . . completely grey. You couldn't tell one from another. It was weird.

I stared at them in amazement.

"A child," said one of the grey men and he gave me a look as if I was some sort of beetle that he'd like to crush.

"Worse still," said the second grey man, "a boy."

"Where are your parents, boy?" rapped out the third grey man in a voice as sharp as barbed wire.

I ran back to the telly room, but, instead of waiting at the door, the three grey men marched after me. I was getting a bit nervous by this time I can tell you. Well, wouldn't you be if your house had been invaded by three identical grey men who didn't like children and especially boys?

Mum and Dad stood up when they saw the three grey men. They looked puzzled and worried.

"What's going on?" said Dad.

"Is it trouble?" asked Mum.

The three identical men stood in a line, opened their identical briefcases and produced three identical cards in identical plastic folders. Mum and Dad looked at them.

"Oh," said Dad. "You'd better sit down."

"Would you like a cup of tea?" asked Mum.

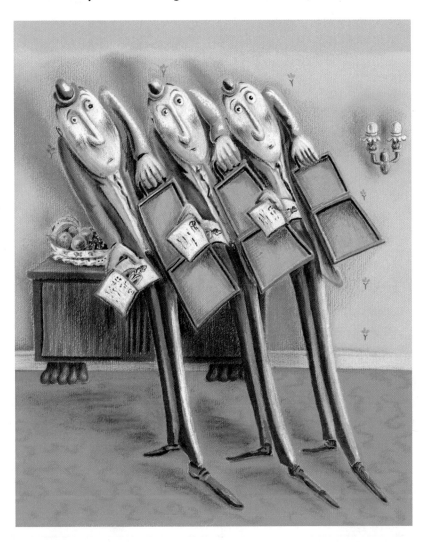

The three grey men didn't reply. They didn't sit down either. Instead they did a funny little dance and recited in unison:

"We're here on official business.

It's a very hush-hush affair.

But we can tell you on the Q.T.,

we have come to do our duty

And are just obeying orders from –" (and here they all jabbed their fingers up towards the ceiling) "– up there.

Yes, we're just obeying orders from up there."

Ella came and stood next to me. "I don't like them," she said in a loud whisper. "Who are they?"

"Sh!" said Mum.

"We're the ones who make sure everything's in order," they continued.

"We're the ones who cross the t's and dot the i's.

We're the ones who have the power to allow a flower to flower

And a tree to grow to regulation size.

And a tree to grow to regulation size."

Then they gave a little bow. Mum and Dad started to applaud, then stopped and looked at each other in embarrassment.

"Daft, I call it," said Ella. I don't think she liked these three grey men. Nor did I, actually.

"They're bonkers," I said, but not too loudly.

"Sh!" said Mum. "Don't be rude, you two."

"Children!" said Dad, giving me a playful smack on my head. "You know what they're like."

"Fortunately not," said Number One Grey Man.

"So what exactly can we do for you?" asked Dad.

"The hole," said Number One. "We've come about the hole."

"What hole?" asked Mum.

"The hole in your garden," said Number Two.

"We don't have a hole in our garden," Dad said.

"Precisely," said Number Three.

"I don't think I understand," said Mum.

"Excellent!" said Numbers One, Two and Three in unison. Then each of them stepped forward and shook hands with Mum and Dad in turn. They completely ignored me and Ella.

"Wait a minute," said Dad.

Number One raised his finger. "Calculations have been calculated," he said, "figures have been totalled, facts have been assembled, the information has been fed into the computer and all the arrows point to one conclusion."

"Your garden," chorused the three grey men.

"For a hole?" said Dad.

"Congratulations!" said the three grey men.

"Are they going to dig a hole in our garden ?" said Ella angrily. She hated to be ignored.

"What for?" I asked.

"What about the apple tree?" Ella demanded.

"And the goldfish pond?" I shouted.

"There's an owl lives in that tree," yelled Ella.

"Ella, Michael. Stop it!" ordered Mum.

"We will be requisitioning the northeast corner only," said Number One.

"What's requisitioning?" I asked. I'd never heard the word before.

"Where's the northeast corner?" butted in Ella.

"Will you two stop asking questions," Dad said sternly. "I can't hear myself think." Then he turned to the three grey men and said, "What I want to know is -."

"Sorry," said Number One. "Top secret."

"Hush-hush," said Number Two.

"Mum's the word," said Number Three.

"I'm flabbergasted," said Mum who was standing there looking - well - flabbergasted.

"Naturally," said Number One.

"But can't you just tell us. . .?" she went on.

"No questions," said Number One.

"Not our department," said Number Two.

"And, of course," said Number Three, "not a word to anyone."

"Not even to the Smiths next door?" Dad asked.

"Especially not to the Smiths next door," said Number One.

"Nor to the Browns across the road," said Number Two.

"Nor to the Fergussons in number 51," said Number Three.

"You see the problem," said Number One.

"What problem?" asked Dad.

"They might all want one," said Number Two.

"A hole?" Mum said.

"Precisely," said Number Three. "A top secret hole."

"Which wouldn't do at all," said Number One.

"Wouldn't it?" said Dad.

"Not enough to go round," said Number Two.

"Holes?" asked Mum.

"Precisely," said Number Three. "And the cost. Think of that."

"I see," said Dad.

But I don't think he did. I don't think he saw any more than the rest of us did. I know that all I could see was Ella getting angrier and angrier, the room getting hotter and hotter, Mum and Dad getting redder and redder and the three grey men getting greyer and greyer.

"You will, of course, be receiving compensation," said the first grey man.

"Compensation?" Dad seemed a bit cheered by that.

"What's compensation?" I asked.

"Which is not our department," said the second grey man.

"I see," said Dad again.

There was an uncomfortable silence, and then the

third grey man said, "Well, if you have no more questions – ."

We all woke up at that and shouted out, "Yes, we do."

"All questions must be addressed to a higher authority," said the three grey men.

"Which higher authority?" we asked.

"All questions must be addressed to a higher authority," repeated the three grey men.

"Where can we find this higher authority?" we demanded.

"All questions must be addressed to a higher authority," said the three grey men again.

There seemed to be no point in asking any more questions after that. We just watched while the three grey men took papers out of their briefcases which they said were plans for the redevelopment of the northeast corner of our garden into a top secret hole and application forms for compensation.

Then they gave a bow and said, "We wish you all a very good day." And were gone. Where they'd been standing I saw three small piles of grey dust. I felt down in the dumps, as if something terrible had happened or was about to happen. I wasn't sure what.

CHAPTER THREE
Ella has a tantrum

Mum and Dad spread the papers on the table and started examining them.

Ella looked at me. "Do you think we're dreaming?" she said.

"What – all of us?"

"Maybe it's just me that's dreaming. It usually is."

"And we're all in your dream, I suppose."

"Precisely," said Ella.

"If I read this right," said Dad, "it's just the top right-hand corner they want."

"That's where the apple tree and the goldfish pond are," said Ella.

"That's not fair," I said.

"You can't let them do it," said Ella.

"Not much we can do," said Dad.

"It's official," said Mum. "That's what they said."

"What's that mean?" I asked. "Official?"

"There are some things," said Dad, "children can't be expected to understand."

"But it's not fair," I said again.

"What do they want to dig a hole for anyway?" Ella said.

"Top secret," said Dad.

"Hush-hush," said Mum.

"And don't you two kids go telling anyone," Dad warned. "You heard what they said."

"Well, I think it's stupid." Ella looked as if she was ready to throw a left hook at somebody. I moved away from her in case it was me. "Why can't they dig holes in their own gardens?"

"Someone has to make sacrifices," said Dad.

"And it must be important," said Mum.

"For the country," said Dad.

"We should be proud they chose us," said Mum. But she didn't look proud. Neither of them did. They both looked – what's the word? – flabbergasted.

"At least," said Dad, "they won't be touching my roses. I do draw the line there."

"And I suppose," said Mum, "there's the compensation."

"Maybe enough to buy a new car," said Dad brightly. "If I could only make sense of these application forms."

"You mean," said Ella, stamping her foot, "you mean you're not going to do anything to stop them?"

"Don't be silly," said Mum.

"There are some things," said Dad, "children don't seem to be able to understand."

"Well, I think that's feeble," shouted Ella. "I think that's the feeblest thing I've ever heard. And if you won't do anything to stop them, I will." And she stomped out of the room and slammed the door.

"Oh dear," said Mum. "She's going to have one of her tantrums."

I curled up in a corner of the sofa, feeling too miserable to say anything. The day was spoilt. The holiday was spoilt.

"She'll get used to it," said Dad. "We all do."

"It seems a shame, though," said Mum.

"What does?"

"The apple tree."

"We can plant another one."

"The goldfish."

"That old thing . . . swimming round and round . . . no use to anyone."

"Still," said Mum. "It does seem a shame."

"They've got to learn they can't have things all their own way. The world wasn't made just for them."

"Or us," said Mum.

"We know that," said Dad.

I slipped off the sofa and made for the door. I couldn't bear to listen to any more.

"Aren't you going to say goodnight?" called Mum.

"Goodnight," I said.

CHAPTER FOUR
Voices in the darkness

I was fast asleep and dreaming of spaceships when Ella woke me up. "Sh!" she said. "Listen."

I listened. "I can't hear anything," I said.

"It's coming from the garden, a sort of singing sound. Can't you hear it?"

"I think so," I said, beginning to wake up. "I thought it was in my dream."

"We ought to go and investigate."

"I'd rather go back to sleep," I said.

"Are you frightened?"

"Course not," I said. But I was . . . a bit. So would you be if you'd heard that strange singing sound, more like wailing really. It was weird.

"Come on, then," she said.

"It's the middle of the night," I said.

"Well, I'm going."

Then I saw that she was fully dressed and was carrying a torch.

"Suppose it's a spaceship landed in the garden and aliens are waiting to kidnap you?"

"Suppose it is," she said and started towards the door.

I didn't know what to do. What with the three grey

men and my dream about being carried off by aliens and
this strange singing sound, I didn't want to be left by
myself.

"Wait a minute," I said, scrambling out of bed. "You'll
need me to protect you."

"Get dressed then," she ordered.

Five minutes later, we were creeping out of the back
door into the garden. It was a dark, warm, mothy night.
There was no moon and the wind rustled through the
trees.

"It's coming from over there," said Ella and she pulled
me towards the goldfish pond and the apple tree. The
singing sounds grew louder. We stood between the
goldfish pond and the apple tree and listened. There
were sounds everywhere. The whole world seemed to
be singing. It was as if we were drowning in the strange
singing, drowning in the magical music. I could hardly
catch my breath. Suddenly the sounds flowed away,
leaving behind an empty silence. We looked at each
other. We didn't dare move. We didn't dare make a noise.
Then out of the silence, out of the darkness, a single
voice rose, a husky voice, a creaky voice. We could hear
the words it sang clearly:

"*I am the tree, the apple tree,*
My roots are as old as history.
My arms are bent, my fingers gnarled,
But I breathe life into the world."

"It's the apple tree," I said. "It's singing."

"Apple trees can't sing," Ella objected.

"But I heard it," I said.

"There's something funny going on here," said Ella.

Then another voice broke the silence of the night, a hollowy voice, an echoey voice:

"I am the owl, by night I fly,
  I shake your slumber with my cry,
  And in my starry wonderland
  I rule the air, I ride the wind."

We both looked up into the apple tree and Ella shone the torch into the branches. We could just make out the dim shape of the owl on a branch of the apple tree, its two eyes gleaming down at us. Before either of us could speak, another voice piped up from another part of the garden, a lovely, trilly, bubbly voice:

"I am the goldfish, I adorn
  Cool water where all life was born.
  In golden silence I create
  My rippling circles of delight."

We ran to the goldfish pond, knelt down and peered in. The goldfish was swimming round and round. In the beam of the torch, we could see the ripples it was making on the water.

"I never thought a goldfish could sing," I said.

The goldfish stopped swimming round and round, came to the surface of the water and blew a bubble.

From what I could see, it seemed to be pouting.

"That's the trouble with you humans," said a cross voice from the fishpond. "You think that what you can't hear isn't there, and what you can't see is invisible. But we goldfish are famous for our songs."

"You've upset it," Ella whispered to me.

"I'm sorry," I said. "I didn't know."

"Do all fish sing?" asked Ella.

"This is what fish like to do best," said the fishy voice. "Each fish has a different scale, you know."

"Really?" said Ella, trying not to laugh.

"And we goldfish have a particularly gentle and delicate song, much admired. Not so much for the notes as for the silences in between."

"The silences?" I said.

"Oh yes. Exquisite. They sometimes last for whole lifetimes and stir great ripples of applause."

"Are we dreaming, Ella?" I whispered.

"I don't think so," she whispered back. "I think this is really happening."

"What a pity!" said the voice from the fishpond. "What a pity it is that you've never been able to hear them."

CHAPTER FIVE
Going up

By this time, we wouldn't have been surprised at anything. I wouldn't have been surprised to see our cat come flying through the air, playing the guitar and singing "We all live in a yellow submarine".

"Earth, air and water," Ella said. Then she stood up. "We hear you, tree," she called. "We hear you, owl. We hear you, fish. But what do you want from us?"

And the voices sang out in answer, one after the other.

"What will we do when our home is destroyed?" sang the fish.

"The monster is coming, his great eyes are humming. He'll tear us apart with his iron claws," sang the owl.

"Oh, who will defend us and who will befriend us? He'll swallow us whole with his giant jaws," sang the apple tree.

"What will we do when our home is destroyed?" sang the fish again.

Then all three voices joined together in a song so mournful that I felt like crying.

"A blight will hold our home in thrall,
The flower will fade, the tree will fall,
And nothing more will ever grow
Only the hollow wind will blow."

"We'll defend you," declared Ella in an excited voice. "Won't we, Michael?"

"Oh yes," I said, doubtfully. "But what are we supposed to do?"

"Yes," said Ella. "And where should we go for help?"

"And how can we get there?"

"And what will stop them digging a hole in our garden?"

"And why are they doing it anyway?"

There was a silence . . . a long silence . . . not a sound.

"Sorry," I said. "I forgot. We're not supposed to ask questions."

"Oh no," came the owl's voice from the apple tree. "Questions are splendid inventions. Splendid. I'm all for them."

"And such a good way of finding out answers," added the apple tree.

"Questions," Ella said thoughtfully. "All questions must be addressed to a higher authority. That's what they said. So that's where we should go: the Higher Authority."

"True, true," said the owl.

"But where does this Higher Authority live?" asked Ella.

"Up," I said.

"What do you mean – up?" said Ella.

"Well, if he's a Higher Authority, we'll have to go up to find him," I explained. It seemed obvious to me.

I could see that Ella was just about to tell me I was being stupid when she was interrupted by a voice from the fishpond. "Absolutely," it said. "The boy has brains after all."

"See," I said.

"All right, Clever-clogs," said Ella. "But where's up and how do we get there?"

"We can offer you three gifts to help you on your journey," said the owl.

"Oh good," I said. I was hoping for a spaceship, at least.

"A bubble to help you to arrive," said the fish. And a bubble sailed out of the pond. It glowed blue, pink and green in the light of the torch.

"A feather to help you on your way," said the owl. And a feather floated down from where the owl was perched. Ella reached up and caught it.

"A leaf to help you to return," said the apple tree. And from the tree, a leaf fell and drifted down on the wind. I caught it and put it in my pocket.

"Thank you," we said. But to tell the truth, I think we were both a bit disappointed.

Then again, mingling with the rustling of the wind, we heard voices singing:

"What will we do when our home is destroyed?...
Who will defend us and who will befriend us?...
When they have cast their deadly spell...
And nothing more will ever grow...
Then we will have no place to dwell...
Only the hollow wind will blow..."

The voices became a jumble, then a mumble, then a murmur, then a whisper. Then they faded away altogether. There was silence in the garden.

"A bubble, a feather and a leaf," said Ella. "It doesn't seem much."

"Look," I said, pointing at the bubble. "It's grown."

The bubble was enormous now, an enormous, quivering balloon of a soap bubble. In fact, it was as big as a spaceship. I couldn't understand why it didn't burst.

"A bubble to help us to arrive," said Ella. "Come on," she said, taking my hand. "We'd better do this together."

And together we walked into the bubble. I shut my eyes as we walked through the wobbly, blubbery, bubbly wall. I felt something wet and soapy smear my face and when I opened my eyes, we were inside the bubble.

"It didn't burst," I said. "It must be magic."

There was a whoosh as the wind caught the underside of the bubble and lifted it off the ground. We held on to each other as the bubble rose into the air.

"Up," I said. "We're going up."

PART TWO
Ella's Story

CHAPTER ONE
Grey Dust

Hello. This is Ella. I'm Michael's older sister – older and more sensible. That's why I'm going to tell you the strangest part of this strange story because you might not believe Michael if he told you. He makes things up sometimes, pretends he's been taken away in a spaceship by aliens and things like that. But I don't – so you can believe me.

Come to think of it, being carried in that bubble was a bit like travelling in a spaceship only more scary. I kept thinking the bubble would burst and we'd be left to fall through the air and plunge into the sea like Icarus in the story. I could see Michael was scared, too; he was holding on to me for dear life. But he wouldn't admit it. He never admits to being scared. I think it's because he's a boy and boys aren't supposed to get scared. But they do. I know they do.

The bubble whizzed through the air, driven by the wind and, although the bubble was transparent, I could see nothing outside except a thick, unbroken blackness. Gradually, I became more confident that the bubble wouldn't just go pop like an ordinary bubble so I jumped up and down a few times as an experiment. It felt rather like jumping on a trampoline.

"If you do that again," said Michael, "I'm going to be sick."

I kept still after that until eventually the bubble stopped speeding through the air and started floating gently down. When it landed on solid ground, there was a hiss, like a bicycle tyre going flat, followed by a popping sound, and the bubble was gone, completely gone. I looked around for some trace of it, but there was nothing left.

We seemed to be in a desert. All I could see in any direction was grey dust swirling in the wind. It was as if we'd landed on a flat, grey carpet that went on forever. There was no colour anywhere. It was daylight, but I couldn't see the sun, only a thin, grey light that filtered through the grey, smoky clouds.

"Where are we?" asked Michael.

"How should I know?" I said. I wish Michael wouldn't ask questions like that. Sometimes he seems to think I should know everything.

"Well, wherever it is, I don't like it. It's horrible."

"We're not here on holiday," I said. 'We've come to find the Higher Authority."

"But there's nobody here," objected Michael. 'There's nothing – just all this grey dust and I want to go home."

"Come on," I said. "We'd better start walking."

"Walking? Where to?"

I thought for a moment and while I was thinking, something soft and feathery stroked my fingers. It was the owl's gift. I still had it in my hand.

"Something to help you on your way," I said and threw the feather into the air. Off it floated in the wind. "Follow the feather," I said.

We must have looked a funny sight, chasing after a feather in this great grey pancake of dust. Only there was no one to see us. The sky was empty. There was no sound: no bird song, no birds, not even a sparrow, not even a crow. And a strange thing seemed to be happening.

"I think things are moving towards us," I said to Michael. "We're not walking that fast, and look, there's a wood coming towards us."

"Can't we go home?" Michael said. "I'm hungry."

"Don't be silly," I said.

And it wasn't a wood either. At least, the trees weren't real trees. They were made of some sort of plastic and painted brown, and the green leaves felt like cloth. As the wood swung past us, a hill came into view, a green hill down which a river flowed. As we watched, the hill came nearer and round it a wall grew up, and the hill and the river turned brown and then grey, and on the hill rose a jumble of towers that seemed to be growing taller by the minute.

In no time at all, we were standing next to the wall and above us soared towers of glass and concrete so tall now that they were tearing holes in the sky.

"This must be it," I said. "This must be where the Higher Authority lives."

"Do you think they'll give us breakfast?" asked Michael.

"Of course they will," I said.

"Bacon and egg," said Michael. "Yum yum."

"Toast and marmalade," I said.

"Sausage and chips," said Michael.

"First we've got to find a way through this wall."

"Follow the feather," said Michael.

I'd forgotten the feather. It had drifted away to our right. We ran after it. It came to a stop in front of two archways in the wall. Over the left archway was an arrow pointing down; over the right one, an arrow pointing up.

"Up," said Michael. "We've got to go up."

The feather suddenly darted through the archway on the left, the one that led down under the ground.

Michael gulped. "That can't be right," he said.

"Come on, Michael," I said, taking his hand. "We'd better follow it."

CHAPTER TWO
Start at the bottom

We were falling. We seemed to be in a sort of lift
which was going down . . . and down . . . and down. Just
as we thought we must have gone through the centre of
the earth and would soon be coming out the other side,
the lift stopped with a bump. The first thing I did was to
grab the feather which was suspended in mid-air and put
it in my pocket. We might need that again.

I don't know how to describe the place we were in. It
was vast, like an enormous barn, and filled with
machines and engines of all sorts. Everywhere we looked
wheels were spinning round, pistons were sliding in and
out of cylinders, chains were clanking, rods and levers
were going up and down and backwards and forwards,
carts were rattling along railway lines and people,
dressed in grey overalls, were rushing about in all
directions. Around the walls were hundreds of different-
sized clocks showing different times. Some of them were
ticking away so fast you could see the minute hands
whizzing round. The noise was deafening and there was
a strange smell in the air, like bad eggs.

"It's a factory," shouted Michael.

"I can see that," I shouted back.

"Look at those two men," Michael yelled. "They're not carrying anything."

It was true. They staggered past us looking as if they were holding between them a heavy load, except that there was nothing there. Unless they were heaving along an invisible tree trunk.

"Excuse me," I said to a man who was rushing past. He was stooped over as if he was carrying something heavy on his back, but there was nothing there that I could see.

"Time waits for no man," he said and was gone.

A woman balancing an invisible weight on her head approached.

"Can you help us?" Michael asked.

"You can't stop progress," said the woman and, pointing to a glass tube rising vertically at the centre of the factory, added, "Start at the bottom and work your way up."

Dodging the machines and the carts and the hurrying people, we made our way to the glass tube. Inside it, a moving staircase wound upwards.

"Start at the bottom and work your way up," said Michael.

We stood on the moving staircase which took us up one floor. In front of us was a door marked NOTHING. I pushed open the door and we went in. At the end of the room was another door, but this room was empty – the emptiest room I've ever seen. Full-length mirrors lined the walls, but when we looked in them, we couldn't see our reflections. Nothing.

"Weird," said Michael.

"What do you expect?" I said. "There was NOTHING on the door."

"Nothing to be afraid of," said a voice which nearly made me jump out of my skin.

"Who said that?" Michael whispered.

"Are you afraid of nothing?" said the voice.

"Help!" squealed Michael.

"I didn't know nothing could be so frightening," I said.

We ran to the end of the room, determined to get out of there as quickly as possible. On this door was written FOODERIE so we rushed through it, expecting to find a restaurant or a kitchen or something. Instead, we seemed to be in a museum. There were glass cases all round the room.

"Look at this one, Michael," I said, peering into a glass case. "It says ENGLISH SAUSAGE 1951."

"How about this, then?" Michael pointed to another case. "CUCUMBER SANDWICH 1890."

"SPAGHETTI BOLOGNESE 1972," I said.

"BREAD PUDDING 1944."

"NETTLE SOUP 1815."

"GRASSHOPPER PIE 1995."

"Tasty," I said. "SLUG STEW 1999."

"Yuk," said Michael.

The strangest exhibit of all said HAMBURGER 1992 and showed a picture of a herd of cattle eating a whole forest.

"It's not fair," wailed Michael. "All this food and there's nothing to eat."

"What about that?" I pointed to a slot machine at the end of the room. "The label says BREAKFAST 2050. I've got two 10p coins we could try."

I put the coins in the machine. Out came two coins which looked exactly the same as the ones we'd put in.

"Enjoy," came a voice from the slot machine.

We took a coin each and ate them. Mine was crunchy and tasted of toast and marmalade. Michael swallowed his and thought for a minute. "Bacon and eggs," he said at last.

"Well, that's breakfast," I said. "We'd better move on or we'll never find this Higher Authority."

On the door at the end of this room was written : HOLES. ASSISTANT ASSISTANT ASSISTANT SALES MANAGER.

"Now we're getting somewhere," I said.

The first thing I saw in the room was a clattering machine churning out paper. There was paper everywhere, piled up on the floor, on the chairs, on the cupboards, on the desk.

Sitting behind the desk, poring over the piles of paper and looking at his watch every few minutes, was a small man with a bald head and a grey moustache. He had tufts of hair on his ears and reminded me of one of my teachers at school.

"Password!" he rapped out, peering at us through the piles of paper. I looked at Michael and he shrugged. I had to say something: "Start at the bottom and work your way up."

"It'll do," he snapped back. "Now, rules are rules and the first rule is - ?"

He looked at us questioningly. We said nothing.

"Obey the rules," he said sternly. "And the rules say: One question, one chance. Correct answer, proceed to next square. Incorrect answer, drop down to the hole factory."

"What's the hole factory?" asked Michael.

"Do you know nothing?" said the man, looking at his watch. "Finest holes anywhere. Manufactured here. Sold all over the world. Perfectly formed for the job in hand. Big, small, long, narrow, wide, short. Holes. In the earth. In the sea. In the sky."

"The hole factory," I whispered to Michael. "That must be what those people downstairs were carrying around."

"Holes?"

"Precisely."

"Top secret holes," continued the man.

"That's ours," said Michael.

"No time to waste," said the man. "Question. Gold.

Coal. Oil. Gas. Fly to the moon. The first ingredient is – ?"

I looked at Michael and Michael looked at me. Neither of us wanted to answer in case it was wrong and we'd have to start again at the hole factory. That would be awful.

"Time's nearly up."

"You answer, Ella," said Michael.

I started to panic. It was worse than being at school. My face felt prickly with sweat. I looked inside my head for an answer but there was nothing there. I had a hole in my head. A hole!

"A hole," I blurted out.

"Proceed," said the man and turned his attention to the paper again.

"Whew!" I said. "That was close."

"Well done," said Michael. "But it was a daft question."

We clambered over the paper to the door behind the man. Through the door was a corridor. At the end of the corridor were two doors. One was marked CHILDREN; the other PLAYERS. We didn't hesitate. We went straight through the door marked CHILDREN. We realised almost immediately that this was a mistake, but by then it was too late.

CHAPTER THREE
The Magister

We slid down the chute into the darkness. Our screams tailed away behind us. Michael was in front of me so when we reached the bottom of the chute, I landed in a heap on top of him.

"Here's two more," said a child's voice.

"I feel as if I'm in a game of snakes and ladders," I said, when I'd picked myself up. "Up the stairs and down the chute."

"I feel bruised," Michael complained, rubbing his arm.

"Just in time for the lesson," said the child's voice.

We looked up. The child was a small boy, smaller than Michael. He was wearing grey shorts, grey shirt, grey socks and grey shoes. I suppose that was his school uniform. The hall we were in was crowded with boys and girls all dressed in grey. They were forming themselves into rows and seemed to be waiting for someone to come on to the stage at the end of the hall.

"Lesson? What lesson?" I asked the boy.

"It's the doing what we're told lesson," he replied.

"I hope it's geography," Michael said. "I'm good at geography."

The boy frowned. "No," he said. "We're learning."

"Learning what?" I asked.

"To do what we're told," he said impatiently.

"Yes, but what for?"

"So we can work our way up, of course," he said. "Come on. The Magister'll be here any minute. You'd better line up with me at the back till you've sorted out your proper uniform."

We joined the rest of the children in the back row and watched in amazement as a strange black machine landed on the stage. It had wheels like a car but it also had overhead blades like a helicopter so it could fly. A helicar, I suppose you'd call it. The door of the helicar slid open and a large man stepped out. He was dressed in black and carried a long black stick. He had big bulging eyes and I was sure he was staring at me.

"He's scary," I whispered to Michael.

"Sh!" said the boy. "That's the Magister."

"Silence!" ordered the man in a rasping voice like a rusty tin can. "You know what time it is. Time to do what you're told. That's the rule. No time to waste. No talking allowed. No ball games allowed. No skipping games allowed. No marbles allowed. No peanuts, popcorn or chewing gum allowed. Nothing's allowed in this country. And that's only allowed on Sundays. Otherwise, the only thing that's allowed is silence. Silence is allowed. So when I raise my rod of iron, I want to hear a loud silence."

No one moved or shuffled or spoke. I suppose there was what people call a deafening silence.

"All right," continued the Magister "you may kneel."

All the children knelt down. So did Michael. So did I. What else could we do? We didn't want to be noticed.

"Hands on heads," ordered the Magister. We obeyed. The Magister raised his stick. "Now this is my rod of iron. With this I have the power to castigate anyone who disobeys me. Understand? Anyone who disobeys will be castigated and you know what castigated means, don't you? Castigated means being thrown into a cauldron of boiling oil, being hung, drawn, halved and quartered and then being sent to bed without any supper. That's what castigated means."

"I'm sorry, I don't think he's allowed to do that," I said to no one in particular. I was fed up with having to kneel down with my hands on my head.

"Silence!" exploded the Magister. "All right. Repeat after me. The squares on a hippopotamus are equal to some of the squares in Madame Tussaud's."

"The squares on a hippopotamus are equal to some of the squares in Madame Tussaud's," chanted the children.

That seemed vaguely familiar to me, though it didn't make much sense.

"Who doesn't understand that?" asked the Magister. Nobody moved or spoke.

"If you don't understand that, wave your right foot in

the air. If you do understand that, wave your left foot in the air. If you don't know whether you understand or not, wave both feet in the air. If you're not waving your feet, stand on your head. If you can't stand on your head, stand on someone else's head..."

By this time, all the children were doing different things. Some were waving a foot in the air. Some were standing on their heads. Some were standing up and trying to wave both feet in the air at the same time and falling backwards on their bottoms. Some were climbing onto other children's heads.

"Bonkers," said Michael and looked desperately at me. "What should we be doing?" he asked.

"Well, I'm not going to be made to look like an idiot."

"If you don't do what you're told," said the boy who had first spoken to us and who was now trying to balance himself on his head, "you'll never work your way up."

"How long does that take?" I asked.

"Ages," said the boy. "Some children never learn."

"I'm not surprised," I said, "if they're told to do such stupid things. Anyway, we can't wait that long. We've got to get to see the Higher Authority or they'll dig a hole in our garden."

"What's a garden?" said the boy, waving both feet in the air.

"A garden? You know . . . with grass and flowers and birds and trees."

"And a goldfish pond," added Michael.

The boy's upside-down face looked puzzled.

"I've heard of those things," he said, "but I've never seen them."

"Don't they have them here?" asked Michael.

"I don't know. I don't think so. We're not allowed out, you see. You're only allowed out if you're driving a machine. And then you've got to be a Player."

"What's a Player?"

"When you've learned to do what you're told, you can be a Player."

"What do Players do?"

"Play parts."

"You mean like actors?" asked Michael.

"I mean like tree painters or hole carriers or machine drivers. Or magisters."

By this time, the boy's face was as red as a beetroot, and I was worried that all his blood was pouring into his brain. Besides, I was tired of talking to an upside-down face. So I gave him a little push and he toppled over. Almost immediately, I felt a rap on my shoulder and the sharp voice of the Magister seemed to cut right through me.

"What have we here?" he said. "Intruders? Troublemakers? Wasting time? Sowing confusion?"

I took hold of Michael's hand and we both turned to face him.

"Please, sir," I said, "we don't belong here. We've just come to see the Higher Authority."

There was a terrible silence. The children stopped what they were doing and turned to watch. The Magister's face was a mask of stone from which his eyes were glaring. He pointed his iron rod at us and said, "The Higher Authority indeed! What impudence! What unholy impudence! You must be castigated. One year in the Nothing Room should do the trick."

At the mention of the Nothing Room, a cold shiver ran down my spine and I saw Michael's eyes widen in fear.

"Let's make a run for it," I whispered.

We bolted. The children made space so we could run between them.

"Stop them!" bellowed the Magister behind us.

They all got up and scrambled after us, but somehow they were getting in each other's way and in the way of the Magister so that they hardly seemed to be moving, and we were able to climb onto the stage where the helicar was parked.

"In the helicar," a voice piped out from somewhere.

Without thinking, we jumped into the strange black machine. The door closed automatically and a panel at the front lit up. There was no steering wheel or anything like that, just buttons. One of them said FLYRISE AUTOMATIC, so I pressed it. There was a whirring sound and the helicar rose in the air. The last sight I had from the helicar windows was of the Magister, surrounded by a throng of struggling children, waving his stick and trying to reach the stage. I think some of the children were still standing on their heads.

CHAPTER FOUR
Up to the Higher Authority

The helicar rose vertically between dimly lit, smooth white walls that were as round as a giant pipe. It seemed to me we were travelling upwards through a hole in the ground.

"Do you know what we're in?" I asked Michael who was staring, fascinated, at the panel of buttons.

"A hole?" he said.

"Precisely."

"It's great, almost as good as a spaceship. But I wonder where we're going?"

"We can't steer it anyway," I said. "So we'll have to go where it takes us."

As I spoke, the helicar popped out of the hole, and for the first time we could see the city we were in. We were rising beside an enormous tower made of dark glass and white concrete and all around us were other towers – so many of them and so tall that the light at ground level was shadowy, dim and grey. Perfectly straight, white roads connected the towers, and we saw black helicars, identical to ours, driving along them. Other helicars were going straight up or straight down next to the tall towers. And wherever there was no road, there were, at intervals

in the grey earth, hundreds of holes, all exactly the same size. Over some of these holes, a white vapour was floating. We couldn't see any people. There was no place for them anyway. Nowhere for them to walk. There were no birds either, as far as I could tell. There was no grass or trees or flowers – and no colours, no colours at all. Everything was black or white or grey.

"Do you think people live in these towers?" asked Michael.

"Or under the ground," I said.

"No gardens," said Michael sadly. "No gardens anywhere."

The helicar stopped rising and hovered alongside the top of the tower.

"I wonder what we do to make it land," I said.

We looked at the panel of buttons. Most of them were labelled DRIVECONNECT, followed by a number.

"All the towers have numbers," said Michael. "So those buttons are to tell the helicar which tower to drive to."

"How do you know?"

"Obvious," he said.

Michael can be really infuriating sometimes. You wouldn't think he was two years younger than me. But I resisted the temptation to thump him. It wasn't the right time to be picking a fight with my brother. We had to stick together.

"That one says RETURNBASE," I said. "I think that must be the one."

Michael pressed the button quickly. He'd been itching to press a button the whole time we were in the machine. A large window in the tower to the side of us slid open. The helicar flew like a giant flying beetle inside the window, landed gently on the floor and switched itself off. The window slid shut again. We were at the top of the tower.

"He's got to be here," I said, as we climbed out of the helicar. "The Higher Authority. He's got to be here at the top of the tower."

We were in a large hangar. There were seven other helicars there, exactly like ours. There was only one door in the hangar, a large metal door with no handle and no way of opening it as far as we could see.

"The door must be guarding a special room," Michael said. "Perhaps that's the room where the Higher Authority lives."

"But how do we get in?" I said irritably. Michael's know-all way of talking was getting on my nerves, and it was upsetting to be so near and yet so far.

"Shall we bang on the door?"

"Better not, that might make somebody angry. We don't want to be arrested or sent to the Nothing Room."

"The Higher Authority might do that anyway. How do we know he'll listen to us?"

"I'm sure he would if we explained. Anyway, it's our only hope."

"Not much of a hope," said Michael. "Especially if we can't get in there to see him."

"I suppose we cheated," I said, "coming up here by helicar. We didn't do what we were supposed to."

"You mean –"

"Start at the bottom and work your way up," we chorused.

There was a buzzing sound and the metal door slid upwards.

"Three cheers!" I said, almost dancing with delight. "That was the magic password."

"Yes," said Michael. "It must have activated the door-opening mechanism."

I looked at him warningly. This was no time to show off. We crept into the room. There was nobody there – no human person, that is – only a giant computer with rows of keys and a large screen which practically filled the room. Michael's eyes gleamed.

"Great!" he said. "Can I have a go?"

"We're not here to play computer games, Michael. It's the Higher Authority we want."

I think we both had the same idea at the same moment. What if the computer <u>was</u> the Higher Authority? It could be. After all, the computer would know everything, much more than any human person. You couldn't get a higher authority than a computer, especially a big one like this.

"It must have the information about the hole in our garden," Michael said. "If we could only find it, we could..."

We looked at each other. "Michael," I said. "You're a genius."

He blushed. I'd never called him a genius before. I'd called him all sorts of things, but never a genius.

We sat ourselves down in front of the computer and set to work. It was easy enough to start. A list of options went up on the screen.

"It's got to be a document," said Michael.

"How about 'Revise Documents'?" I said.

We pressed that key. Another list appeared on the screen. We didn't have to look far. "Holes Top Secret" was right at

the top of the list. We keyed it in, and a list of places went up on the screen. We scanned it carefully for our address. It wasn't there. We rolled the page down, and down, and down.

"All those top secret holes," I said. "What do they need them for?"

"We're probably at the bottom," said Michael.

He was right. At the end of the list was our address: 37, Waterboard Road. We managed to point the cursor at it.

"Now," I said. "All we've got to do is find a way to delete it."

At that moment, a loud noise like a police siren made us jump out of our seats. It seemed to be coming from outside and inside the building.

Michael looked at me, startled. "That's for us," he said. "They're after us."

"Quick," I said. "We must find the 'delete' key."

We looked at the rows and rows of keys. Most of them had symbols which we didn't recognise at all. The sirens seemed to be getting louder.

"We'll never find it," said Michael. "They'll find us first and we'll be arrested and put in the Nothing Room or something even more horrible."

"Come on, Michael," I said. "We can't give up now. One of those keys must delete."

We looked at them all again with their strange symbols.

"What about that one?" I said. "It doesn't have anything on it at all. Nothing."

Michael shrugged. "I don't know," he said. "It could be anything."

"Shall I try it?"

He nodded. I thought I could hear the sound of people rushing towards the door which led to the other parts of the building. The wailing sirens were so loud they seemed to be right inside my head.

I pressed the key. The machine shook and groaned. Then to our amazement, it spoke. "ARE YOU SURE?" it said.

"Yes," we yelled and keyed in a Y. Our address vanished from the screen.

"Mission accomplished," shouted Michael, switching the machine off. We rushed out of the room into the hangar and climbed inside our helicar. Before I could catch my breath, Michael pressed a button in the panel.

"What did you do?" I shouted at him.

"Don't worry," he said. "I know what I'm doing."

The window in the hangar slid open, the whirring helicar slid through it and started to descend.

"Look down there," I told Michael.

The straight white roads below were lined with

helicars looking like armies of black beetles on the march. They were converging on our tower. We could still hear their sirens above the whirring noise of our own helicar.

We landed at the foot of the tower. There was nowhere we could drive to because all the roads were blocked with the wailing black beetles, so we scrambled out. The air outside was warm and muggy. It had an unpleasant smell which made my head swim. There was a taste of dust on my tongue.

Michael wrinkled up his nose. "Yuk," he said. "What do we do now?"

I fished the feather out of my pocket. "Follow the feather," I said.

The feather led us off the road onto the grey dust where all the holes had been drilled. The white vapour that was drifting out of some of them was making me feel sick and Michael started to cough. The good thing was that no one seemed to be following us. No one emerged from the helicars which were now assembled at the foot of the tower and which appeared to be watching us.

"I don't think they're allowed out of their helicars," I said.

"I'm not surprised," said Michael. "This is worse than being on the moon. We ought to have filter masks."

Suddenly the feather dipped over a hole instead of

leading us round it and then dived down it, disappearing into the darkness. We peered down into the hole, though there was nothing to see.

"A leaf to help you to return," I said.

Michael felt in his pocket and brought out the leaf from the apple tree. I knew it wasn't an ordinary leaf because it was still a fresh green colour. Michael placed it on the dust at the edge of the hole and looked at it doubtfully.

"I don't believe in travelling by leaf," he said.

"Well, I don't believe in travelling by spaceship," I said. "Or walking on the moon."

"That's different," Michael said.

Even as we were arguing, I could see the leaf growing bigger and bigger, and thicker and thicker. Soon it was a large, green, leaf-shaped carpet with the edges curled upwards.

"We'd better believe in it," I said, "because we haven't any choice."

We stepped onto the leaf, held hands and closed our eyes. I felt the leaf slip into the hole and float very gently downwards, just like a leaf falling from a tree, I thought to myself. It was a pleasant, dreamy sensation, floating down and down and down. And we saw nothing and felt nothing and heard nothing until ...

CHAPTER FIVE
Home

We opened our eyes. We were standing under the apple tree in our own garden. A gentle wind rustled through the leaves. It was still night – a warm summer's night with no moon. It seemed that no time at all had passed since we'd soared upwards in that magic bubble on our way to save the fish, the owl and the tree from being destroyed. We looked at each other. We'd been through a lot, me and my brother. He seemed to me bigger and older than before, though I know he couldn't really be. It's just that he seemed less of a silly little nuisance now, more of a friend. I was glad I had him as a brother.

"Bed," I said. "If we creep in very quietly, they'll never know anything. We'd better not tell them. They'll never believe us anyway."

Michael yawned. "I won't say a word," he said.

The rest of the summer holidays passed without any of us mentioning the three grey men and their plans for the garden. We didn't want to talk about it to Mum and Dad, and they didn't seem to want to talk about it either. Perhaps they hoped it was all a bad dream which would go away if they ignored it. Perhaps they'd forgotten all about it. Perhaps wiping the plan for our garden from the computer had also wiped it from their memories. I don't know. Anyway, not a word was said about it afterwards, though I half expected those grey men to turn up on the doorstep any moment, and we all seemed unusually nervous whenever there was a ring at the door. But the three grey men never came back. Once we heard Mum and Dad talking about a plan to widen the road at the end of our garden, but they told us it was probably just a rumour.

On the last day of the holidays, I was lying under the apple tree playing snakes and ladders with Michael. Just for a change, we were going up the snakes and down the ladders, but we still didn't manage to finish the game. Dad's roses looked beautiful in the bright sunshine and there was a pleasant breeze to keep us cool.

"School tomorrow," I said.

"Yes," said Michael. "It was a good holiday though, wasn't it?"

"Well, we didn't exactly go anywhere on holiday, did we?"

"Not on holiday, no. But we did go somewhere – somewhere no one else knows about. That was an adventure."

"And we saved the owl and the goldfish and the apple tree from being destroyed."

"Do you think they'll come back, those grey men?" said Michael.

I shrugged. "I hope not," I said.

"What will you do if they do come back? What will you do if they still want to make a top secret hole in our garden?"

"I won't let them," I said. "I won't let them do it."

"Nor me," said Michael.

There was a long, long silence and then Michael raised himself onto his elbows as if he was listening for something.

"What's the matter?" I asked.

He looked at me and smiled. "I thought," he said, "I heard a goldfish singing."